I WANT TO BE SPAGHETTI!

written by KIERA WRIGHT-RUIZ
illustrated by CLAUDIA LAM

Kokila

I am Ramen, but I want to be spaghetti
because everybody loves spaghetti!

Down their aisle, I see so many people picking from boxes and boxes of spaghetti. Everywhere I look, there is some story about spaghetti—what goes on it, where it's from, and how tasty it is.

The ramen aisle is so much smaller. Why is there no story about us? It's not the same.

Spaghetti is everywhere.
Maybe if I were more like spaghetti,
I'd be everywhere too.

Is it because
penne is shorter?

Or angel hair
is thinner?

Maybe it's
because fettuccine
is wider.

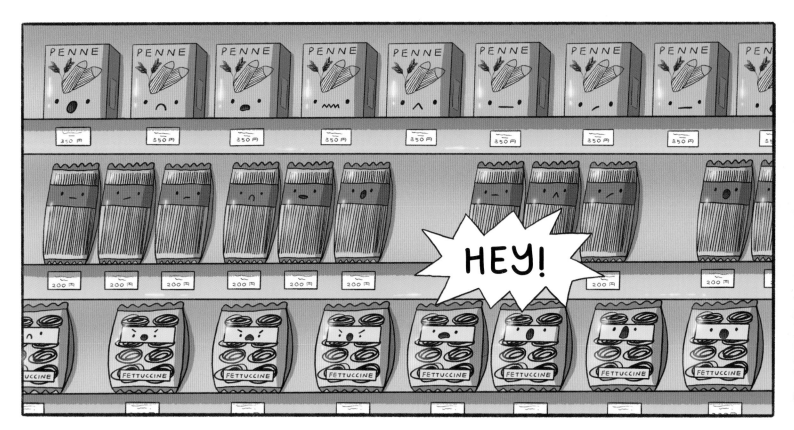

Ramen is so square,

and our noodles have too many curves.

But I think if I tried,
I could be like spaghetti too.

STRETCH
STRETCH
STRETCH

I hope I get to
become spaghetti.

Maybe they'll put meatballs on me.

Or tomato sauce!
Cheese! And herbs!

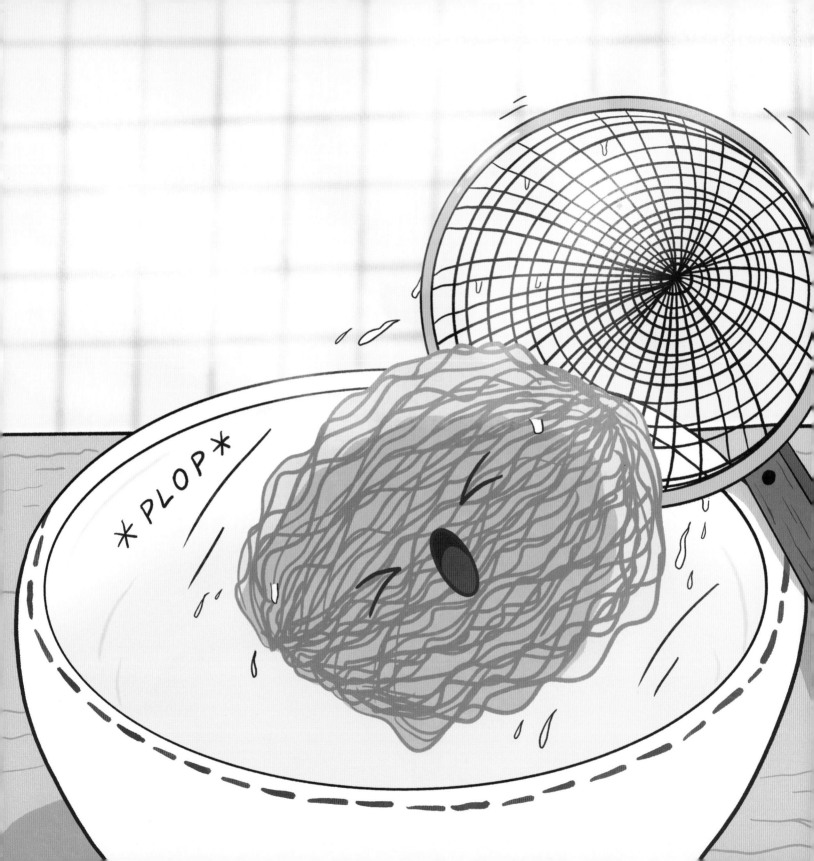

This isn't what's
supposed to
happen!

But wait,

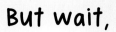

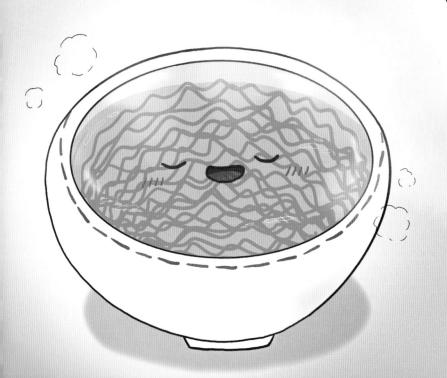

it's so warm . . .
and cozy.

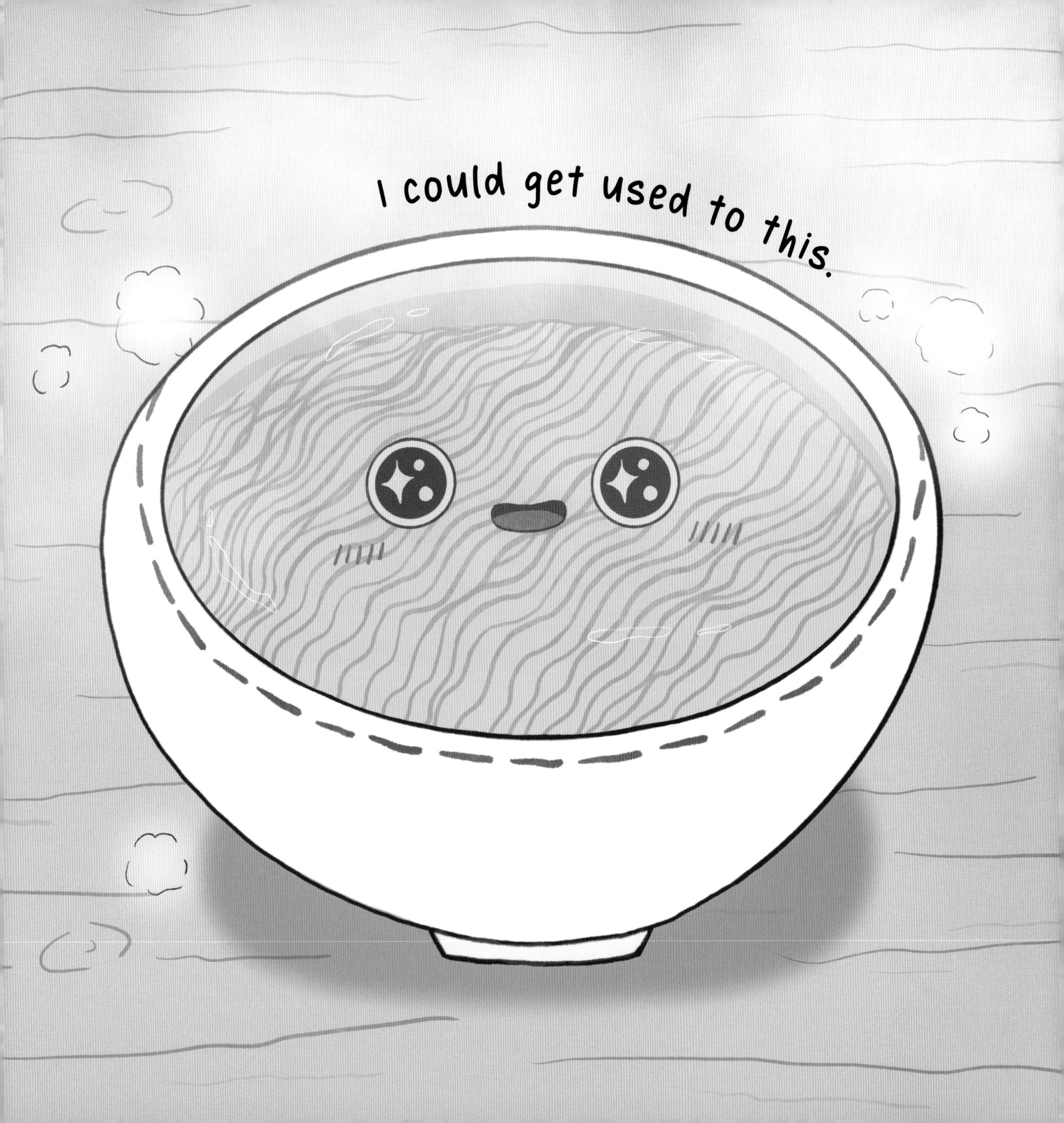
I could get used to this.

Are you like meatballs?

I've seen those in pictures of spaghetti.

Could it be
tomato sauce?

What are you doing here?

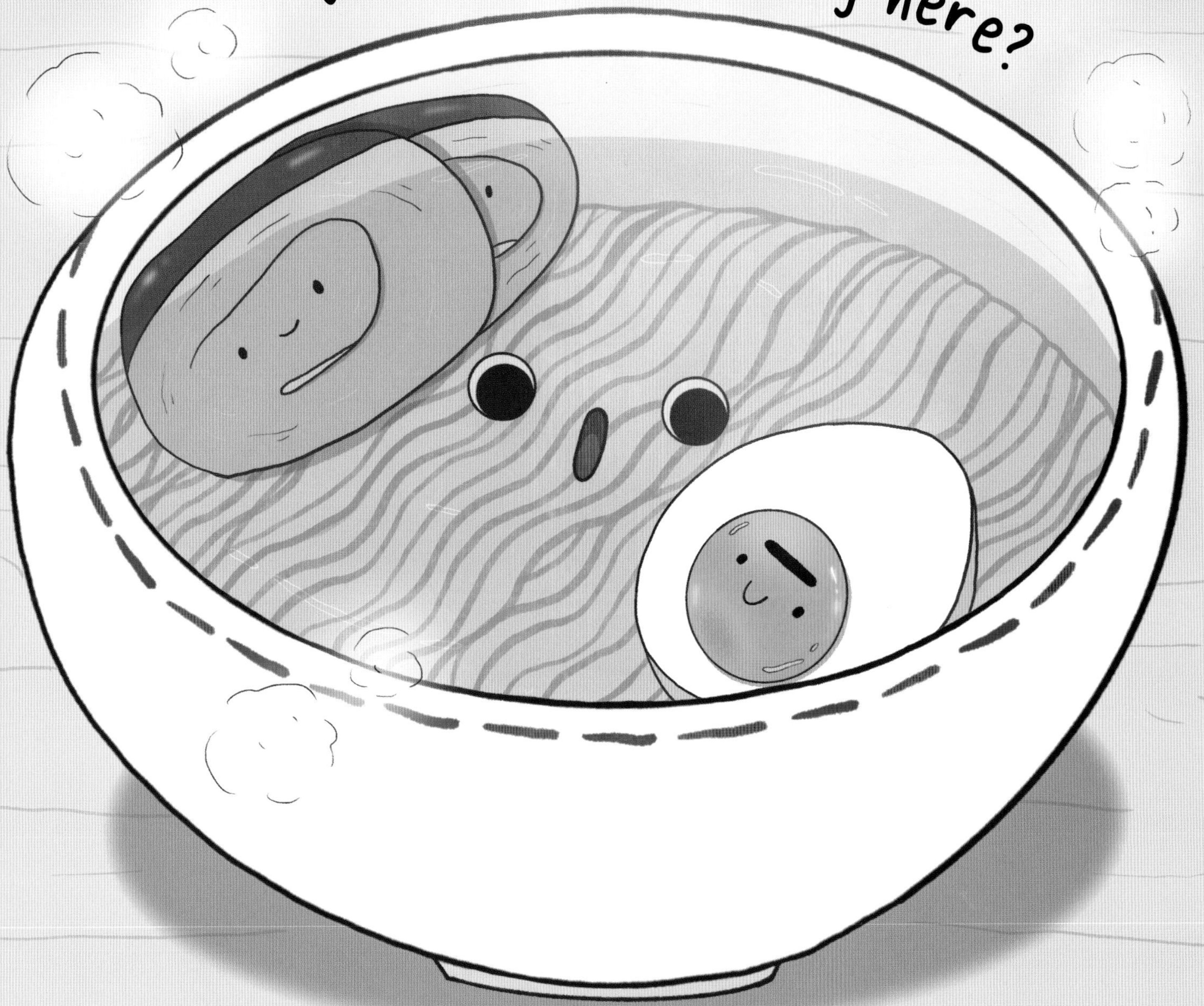

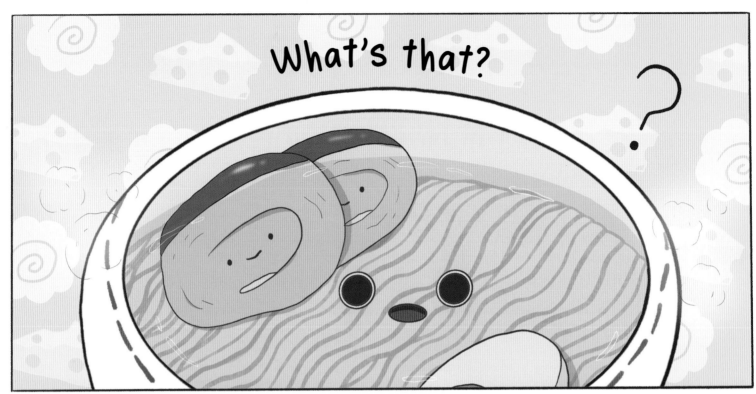

Whether you're

square,   curvy,   short,

or long, we're all beautiful
in our own way.

Thanks to each of you,
I know how to be myself!

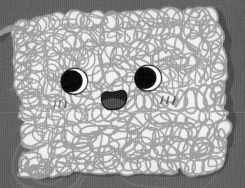

Spaghetti is good, but I am happy because . . .

I am Ramen!
And ramen is
perfect just
the way
it is.

Author's Note

The history of noodles is a long one. The oldest evidence of them was found in China, where people dug up a bowl of noodles that was over four thousand years old. It suggests that the world-famous dish was invented in Asia, and over time it spread across the world. It wasn't until 1958 that instant ramen noodles were invented in Japan by Momofuku Ando, who is known as the father of instant noodles.

When Japan was experiencing food shortages after World War II, Momofuku created something he thought could help solve world hunger: flash-fried ramen noodles. They could be packaged for a long period of time and cooked quickly—or in an "instant"—in hot water.

Today, instant noodles are popular worldwide. Korean Shin Ramyun, Indian Maggi, Brazilian Turma da Mônica, Italian Saikebon—there are countless brands and flavor variations out there. While this story has Japanese elements, every kind of instant ramen is delicious and special. Noodles are a source of pride for people all over the world, but in particular Asia, which is how our little Ramen character came to be.

This story is based on my experience growing up thinking that I looked too different to be accepted. But it was never true. I hope wherever you are right now that you know this: You are perfect as you are—just like a warm bowl of ramen.

—Kiera

For Thor and Ben.
—K. W. R.

For Steven and Marco.
—C. L.

KOKILA
An imprint of Penguin Random House LLC, New York

First published in the United States of America by Kokila, an imprint of Penguin Random House LLC, 2023

Text copyright © 2023 by Kiera Wright-Ruiz
Illustrations copyright © 2023 by Claudia Lam

Visit us online at penguinrandomhouse.com.

Library of Congress Cataloging-in-Publication Data is available.

Manufactured in China
ISBN 9780593529874

3 5 7 9 10 8 6 4
TOPL

This book was edited by Sydnee Monday and designed by Jasmin Rubero.
The production was supervised by Tabitha Dulla, Nicole Kiser, Ariela Rudy Zaltzman, and Cherisse Landau.

Text set in Hynings Handwriting V2 and Dreaming Outloud
Hand lettering by Claudia Lam

The art for this book was made digitally, making use of various forms of brush strokes such as ink pen,
pencil, crayon, and dry brush to create a mixed-media style that effectively illustrates the vibrancy
of supermarket aisles, product packaging, and Ramen's vivid imagination.